This **Picture Mammoth** belongs to

_____

_____

Wolf!

Sara Fanelli

FOR
MARIO & LINUCCIA
J.B. & EMILY
papá GION & mamma ROSALIE

5·94   8·95   1·96

First published in Great Britain 1997
by WH Books Ltd and Mammoth
imprints of Reed International Books Limited
Michelin House, 81 Fulham Road, London, SW3 6RB
and Auckland, Melbourne, Singapore and Toronto

Copyright © Sara Fanelli 1997
Sara Fanelli has asserted her moral rights
Typography by Claire Harvey

ISBN 0 7497 2870 1

A CIP catalogue record for this title
is available from the British Library

Produced by Mandarin Offset Ltd
Printed and bound in China

&

It was a

lovely sunny day and Wolf decided to go for a walk into the city to make some new friends

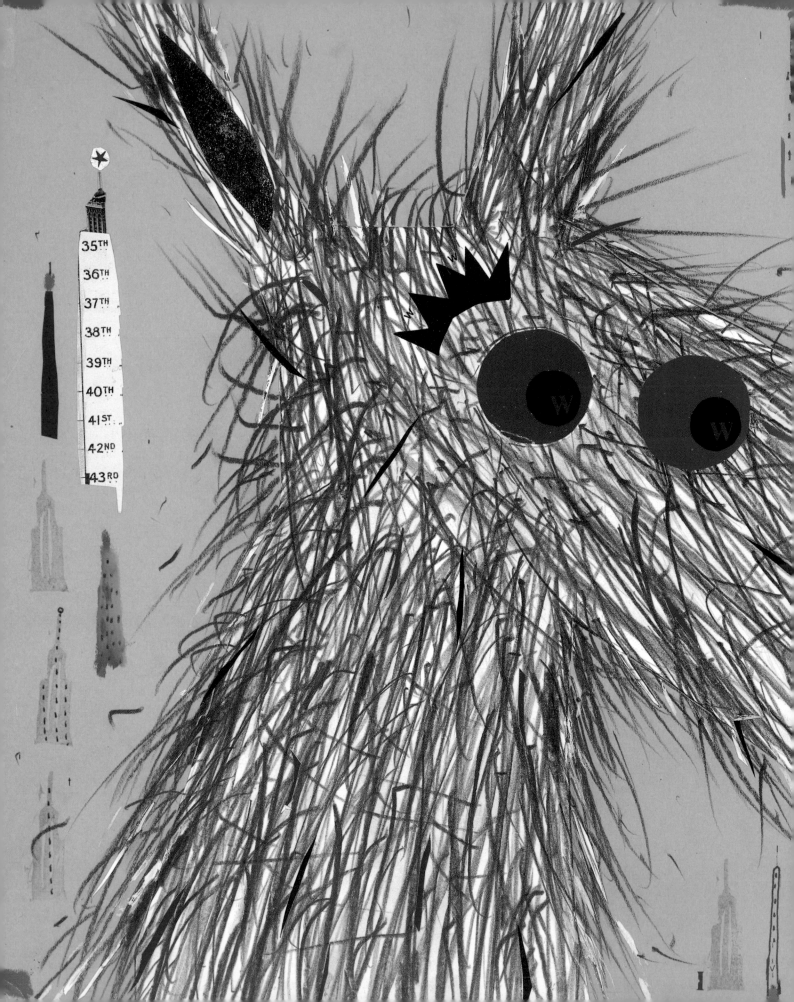

35TH
36TH
37TH
38TH
39TH
40TH
41ST
42ND
43RD

On
the
road
Wolf met
an old lady
searching for her
spectacles.

Wolf tried to be helpful
and found them for her.
But, after she had put
them back on and could
see again, she peered at
Wolf and ran away in
fright. Wolf was sorry
she had not stayed
for a chat.

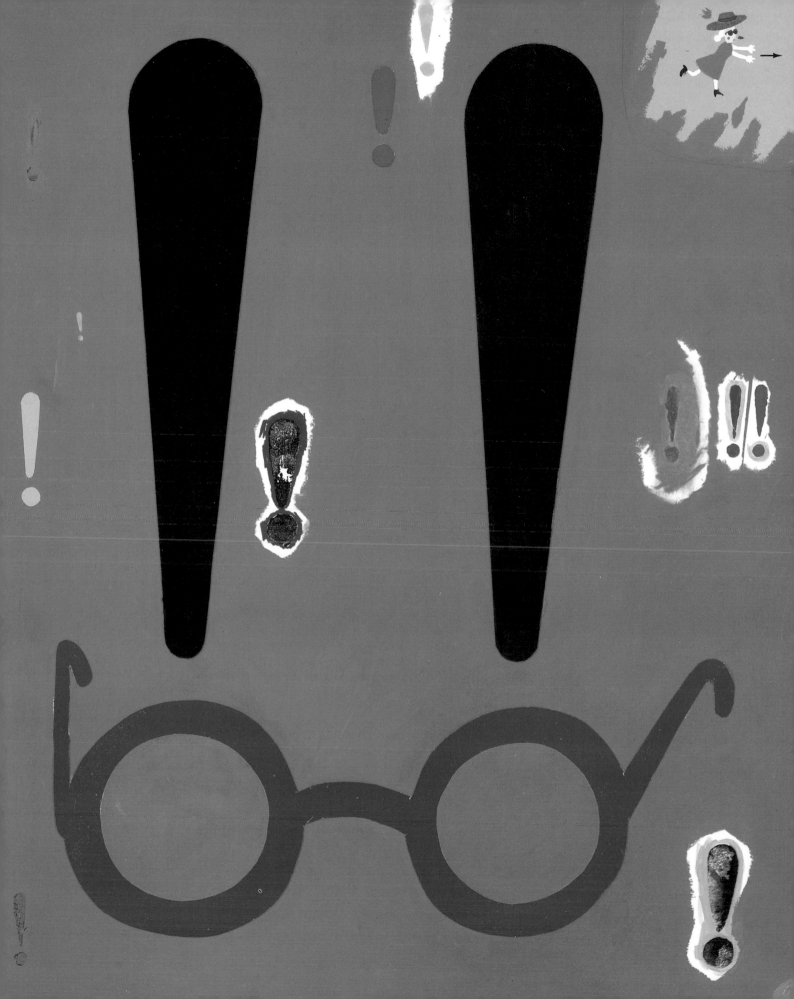

Further on,
Wolf saw a **big** bright car that
a man was busily repairing.

Wolf wanted to help him too and began handing him the tools.

After the job
was finished,
the man stood
with a startled
look and

Next Wolf came upon a group of children playing with masks. They thought that he too was wearing a mask and asked him to join the game.

Wolf was so happy and enjoyed playing with them.

But Something Went Wrong.

For, when the children

took off **their masks,**

they realized Wolf did not have one on.

So they ran **away**

as fast as they could.

Wolf was very sad because they
did not want to be his friends.
However, he had an idea.

Maybe
if he did
wear a mask
he could
make
some
friends

Then a barber saw him and thought
Wolf needed a shave.
He invited him into his shop.

s, s'il vous plait.

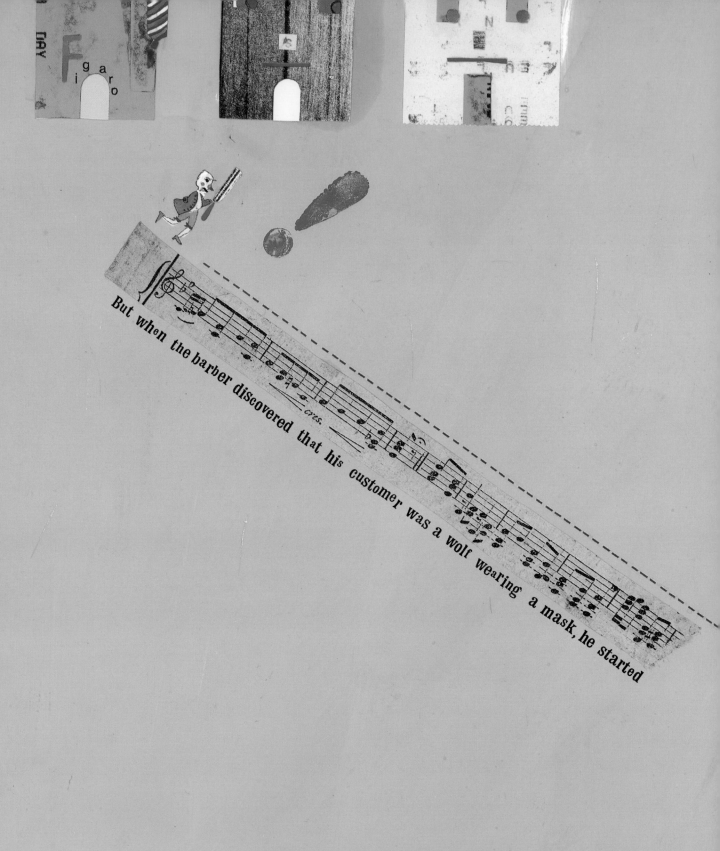

But when the barber discovered that his customer was a wolf wearing a mask, he started

chasing after Wolf with his razor!
Running fast to
escape, Wolf finally
reached a garden
where he stopped
to hide and to
catch his breath.

But very soon the gardener arrived

and started watering the plants.

And Wolf had to
start running
again.
It seemed
everyone
was after him.

Wet and alone, Wolf

felt sad. He had tried

35

to be   friendly   but   everyone   he'd

met   had found   him   fierce   and   scary.

It was his friend Rosie
and Wolf told her about
his many misadventures
and misunderstandings.

All the people
he had met in the city
were astonished to hear his words.
They suddenly realized

Vous voilà,

bien instruite sur tou

how wrong
they had been to think
Wolf was a ferocious creature.
Really he was very amiable !

So they followed the two wolves into the forest and together,

they all had a wonderful picnic.

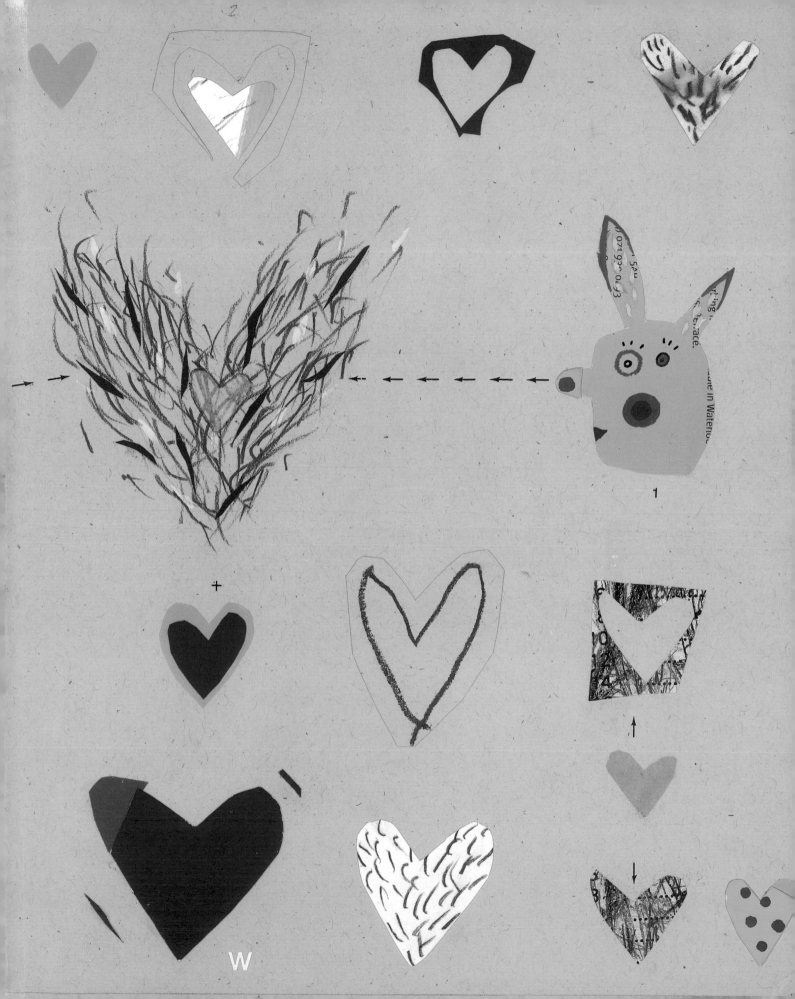

Seven of the Best

Cat's Colours
Jane Cabrera
ISBN 0 7497 3120 6

Do Pigs Have Stripes?
Melanie Walsh
ISBN 0 7497 3026 9

Ella and the Naughty Lion
Russell Ayto and Anne Cottringer
ISBN 0 7497 3019 6

I Like It When
Mary Murphy
ISBN 0 7497 3119 2

When Martha's Away
Bruce Ingman
ISBN 0 7497 2957 0

Mouse Creeps
Reg Cartwright and Peter Harris
ISBN 0 7497 3123 0

Wolf
Sara Fanelli
ISBN 0 7497 2870 1

picture mammoth